Winnie the Pooh
Growing Up Stories

Stories by Kathleen W. Zoehfeld
Illustrated by Robbin Cuddy

Ladybird

This edition published in 2002 by Ladybird Books Ltd.
80 Strand, London, WC2R 0RL

Printed in China

www.ladybird.co.uk

Contents

 Introduction

These stories were created as a way of gently introducing new experiences and challenges to young children, guided by Winnie the Pooh and his friends. In the Hundred-Acre Wood, children will find a world of imagination, friendship and new discoveries.

Tigger's Moving Day

For a child, moving house can be an overwhelming experience. A way of easing fears is to give children an active role. When they see themselves as an important part of the events that are unfolding, children will feel much more secure. In our story, Tigger is moving house. He discovers that this involves a range of emotions from anxiety and excitement to security and comfort. A child will enjoy being part of this new experience and can be given the responsibility of packing their favourite things. Hopefully, when safely in their new home, children will see change as exciting, rather than daunting.

🦋 Roo's New Baby-sitter

In this story, the idea of participation and involvement is explored further. Parents know that a good baby-sitter should be sensitive to a child's anxieties of being in the care of someone new. However, a new baby-sitter will be unfamiliar with a child's routines which may increase anxiety further and a level of trust must be gained. A bond can then be slowly formed.

When Kanga introduces Pooh as Roo's new sitter, Pooh discovers that, for the most part, baby-sitting is not sitting at all! Pooh listens to Roo, and tries to learn his routines. Children, missing their parents, may mask their emotions as resentment towards the new sitter. However, play is a universal language and, just as Pooh comes to realise, an important, albeit exhausting, part of baby-sitting!

🦋 Pooh Helps Out

All children must learn the concept of helping. In this story, helping is first presented as an antidote to Pooh's boredom, and ends up being a remarkable series of learning opportunities. Parents allowing their children to help out with household chores are teaching their children valuable skills and routines. Pooh seeks to conquer his boredom by finding someone to do nothing with. He first recruits Piglet, who agrees to do nothing with Pooh as soon as he washes his dishes. The nothing they were planning to share ends up in an activity that Piglet proclaims "the perfect chore for two". Pooh finds that each of his friends would love to do nothing with him, but, like Piglet, have chores to be done first, or problems they need help in solving.

🦋 Pooh's Scrapbook

A scrapbook is a useful reference point for remembering an experience, and an opportunity for children and adults to reveal and share their experiences. In "Pooh's Scrapbook", a rainy day becomes an opportunity for such a project, as Piglet suggests that he and

his Hundred-Acre friends create a Sunny Day Scrapbook to remember sunny days. Pooh, of course, remembers climbing a tree for honey. Tigger recalls making castles in the sand. The making of the scrapbook is not only an enjoyable way to spend a rainy day, but also an opportunity for children to discuss different memories.

🦋 Pooh Welcomes Winter

The concept of the four seasons can come alive for children through experiences that offer direct discovery. Children learn the markings of time, not only by a height chart on the wall, but by collected memories.

Winter means snow melting on the tongue, cold hands in warm mittens and hot cocoa. As Pooh and his friends know, winter is a joyous time; a time for play, a time for discovery, and a time for friends.

In "Pooh Welcomes

Winter", Pooh and friends are delighted by the first snow. Filled with their usual enthusiasm, they head off in search of Winter, in order to welcome him. They mistake Christopher Robin's snowman for Winter and invite him to sit in Pooh's chair by the fireplace. Happily, Christopher Robin comes along to save the day – and his snowman! Winter finally does arrive and is warmly greeted.

Be Patient, Pooh

Waiting isn't easy. To children, waiting for something, such as a birthday, can seem interminable.

In this story, Pooh is awaiting his birthday party that evening, and must get through the day until the time arrives. He tries to pass the time as best he can and discovers that waiting is much easier when he's with friends. Eventually, Christopher Robin reads him a story, and before long, it's time for the party to begin! Young children will learn, with Pooh, that the busier you are, the quicker time will fly by!

Tigger's
Moving Day

"Tigger, you don't have enough bouncing room in this little house," said Rabbit when he came visiting one day.

Plunk! A toy truck teetered off the shelf and landed on Tigger's head. "Ouch," he said, "it's true. But what can I do?"

"We've got to find you a bigger house," declared Rabbit. "That's all there is to it!"

"But . . . " said Tigger.

"No buts," said Rabbit. "I'm going to organise the others right away. Don't worry – we're going to find you a new home!"

By the end of the day, they had found the perfect place, and everyone felt very excited.

"It IS a bouncy house," said Tigger. "The kind of house Tiggers like best!" He bounced and bounced, and he didn't bump into anything.

"But," he said, sighing, "I'll miss my old house. And I won't live next door to little Roo any more. I'll miss him, too."

"I know you'll miss being neighbours with Kanga and Roo," said Christopher Robin, "but now you'll live much closer to me. We can have fun being neighbours – just like you and Roo did."

"Do you like to bounce?" asked Tigger.

"Sometimes," said Christopher Robin.

"Besides, dear," said Kanga, "I promise to bring Roo over to visit, just as often as you like."

"Well, then," said Tigger, perking up a bit. "I hope everyone can stay awhile. We can play a game together and eat some cookies."

Tigger looked in his new kitchen. No cookies. He opened his new cupboard. No games.

"It's sort of empty, isn't it?" said Eeyore.

"Mmm," agreed Tigger. "Tiggers don't like empty houses. I like my old house better."

Rabbit put his paws on his hips and stared at Tigger. "We haven't finished yet. We need to move all your things from your old house to this house," he said.

"Everything?" asked Tigger.

"Every last little thing," said Rabbit, "and that's a big job, so we'll start first thing tomorrow morning."

Rabbit told everyone to bring all the boxes they could find to Tigger's house.

"Wow! Boxes are fun!" cried Roo. "Look at me jumping!"

Tigger and Roo bounced in and out of all the boxes.

"There'll be time for fun later," scolded Rabbit. "Now we've got to pack Tigger's things."

The next morning, back at his old house, Tigger packed all his games and his stuffed animals in a box. He took his favourite lion out and hugged him. "I want you to stay with me."

Rabbit packed Tigger's dishes.

Kanga packed Tigger's clothes.

Pooh and Piglet packed Tigger's food.

Soon Eeyore arrived with his donkey cart. "We can use this to haul your bigger things," he said helpfully, "furniture and whatnot."

Christopher Robin and Owl hoisted Tigger's bed and table and chairs onto the cart.

Owl and Gopher loaded the boxes.

"Time to go!" cried Rabbit.

Everyone pulled and pulled.

"Now my new home will be perfect!" cried Tigger, as they unloaded the cart and carried everything inside.

"Thanks for your help, everyone," he cried. "Moving was as easy as pie!"

After his friends had gone, Tigger put his toys on his new shelves.

He pushed his bed under the back window, just where he wanted it.

He set his table and chairs in the middle of the big kitchen.

He put his cereal in the new cupboard.

When he had finished, Tigger sat down to rest. Hmmm. Seems like an awfully quiet house, he thought.

He tried out a few bounces, but decided he wasn't in such a bouncy mood, after all.

"I miss Roo," he said.

Just then, Tigger heard a little voice cry, "Hellooo!"

"Roo!" cried Tigger. "Kanga! Come on in!"

"We've brought you a bag of cookies," said Kanga.

"Oh, yummy!" cried Tigger.

"Hellooo! Hellooo!" Tigger soon heard all his friends calling outside his new door.

Everyone had brought housewarming presents for Tigger.

"Our work's all done," said Rabbit. "Now it's time for fun!"

"Hooray!" cried Tigger as he bounced from room to room with Roo. "There's plenty of room for fun – and friends – in my new house!"

Roo's New Baby-sitter

"Roo, dear, your baby-sitter will be here soon," said Kanga.

"I don't want to be baby-sitted!" cried Roo.

"Roo, I'm just going shopping for a little while," said Kanga. "You'll have fun with Pooh."

"I don't want to have fun!" cried Roo.

"Yes, dear," said Kanga, buttoning her coat.

Roo found a bag and began filling it with things. "But I'd be a BIG help shopping!" he cried.

"Some other time, dear," said Kanga.

"What other time?" asked Roo.

"Well, not this time," said Kanga. "Oh, look! Here comes Pooh now."

"Hello, Pooh," said Roo. "I'm shopping!" He put more things in his bag, partly because this was fun, and partly because he didn't want his mother to see how much he minded being left behind.

"Pooh," said Kanga, "don't let Roo get into any mischief."

"Oh, I won't let him get into anything," said Pooh cheerfully.

"Bye-bye!" Roo and Pooh waved as they watched Kanga hop down the path and over the bridge. When she was out of sight, little Roo didn't look so happy.

Pooh gave Roo a hug and put him in his high chair.

"What you need is a nice smackerel of honey to cheer you up," said Pooh.

"I like shopping," squeaked Roo. "I don't need to eat."

"Hmmmm, doesn't want to eat," said Pooh. "NOW what do I do?"

"Do you know how to baby-sit?" asked Roo.

"Well, yes," said Pooh, "all except the actual baby-sitting part."

"**I**'m good at baby-sitting," said Roo excitedly, bouncing up and down. "I'll tell you how."

Roo took Pooh outside.

"The first thing a baby-sitter does is climb!" cried Roo. "Let's see who can climb the highest, you or me."

Pooh, who had always thought that baby-sitting just involved actual SITTING frowned a little and said, "Okay, let's find a good climbing tree."

They stood under the old apple tree in Roo's back garden. Roo jumped and jumped, but he couldn't reach even the lowest branch.

"Baby-sitters always help," he said.

"I see," said Pooh.

Roo hopped from branch to branch, and Pooh climbed up behind him.

"Mmmm," said Roo. "Look at those apples. Baby-sitters always pick apples for supper."

Pooh clambered up to the highest branch. He picked four bright red apples and tucked them under his arm. Then he inched back down.

"Oh, Pooh," cried Roo. "You can climb with one arm!"

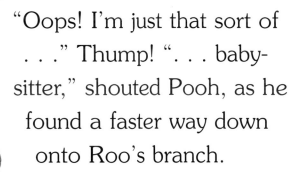

"Oops! I'm just that sort of . . ." Thump! ". . . baby-sitter," shouted Pooh, as he found a faster way down onto Roo's branch.

They sat side by side and swung their feet and ate the sweet apples.

"This is the best supper ever!" cried Roo.

"What do baby-sitters do AFTER supper?" asked Pooh.

"They give baths," said Roo, "with LOTS of bubbles."

Roo showed Pooh how baby-sitters pour a whole bottle of bubble bath into the bathwater.

"It seems like a lot," said Pooh.

"Just right," said Roo.

Roo took off his little shirt and hopped in. He disappeared under the bubbles.

"Where's Roo?" asked Pooh, sort of to himself and sort of out loud. "Wfffffff." He blew on the bubbles. He couldn't see Roo anywhere.

He swished his paws through the bubbles. He couldn't feel Roo.

"Look at me jumping," squeaked a little voice. Pooh could HEAR Roo!

"There you are!" cried Pooh.

Roo, all wet and bubbly, was jumping on his bed.

Pooh chased him with the towel and dried him off. "Time for your vitamins," said Pooh, a little more sternly than when Poohs usually say such things.

"I don't want any," said Roo. He folded his arms across his chest and stuck out his chin.

"Oh, well," said Pooh, slumping in a chair. "Why don't you give ME a spoonful?"

"Now, Pooh, dear, here's your medicine," said Roo in a cheerful, grown-up sort of voice.

"Ahhh! Much better," said Pooh. "Thank you, Roo. You are a good baby-sitter."

"I'm baby-sitting!" sang Roo happily.

Kanga opened the door and saw Roo and Pooh snuggled together in the chair.

"Mum! Look at me baby-sitting!" cried Roo. "I'm baby-sitting Pooh!"

"Of course you are, dear," said Kanga.

Pooh Helps Out

Winnie the Pooh sat on the edge of his bed and looked all around his cosy house.

Nothing to do, he thought.

Pooh tried humming a little hum. "Hum de dum," he hummed. "Well, that's a nothing little hum," he said.

After a while, nothing to do began to feel quite bothersome.

Maybe I should find someone to do nothing with, he thought. That would be so much more cheerful.

Pooh knocked at Piglet's door. "Piglet," he said, "I've come to see if you'd like to do nothing with me."

"Oh, I'd like to do nothing," said Piglet, "but first I have to wash my dishes."

Pooh brightened. "Oh, may I help?"

"Yes, indeed!" cried Piglet. He handed Pooh a tea towel. Piglet washed and Pooh dried.

When all the dishes were stacked neat and clean in the cupboard, Piglet said, "Thank you, Pooh. That was the perfect chore for two. Now I'm ready to do nothing."

Pooh hummed. Piglet wiggled his ears and tapped his foot.

Pooh yawned. Then Piglet had to yawn, as well.

"Pooh?" Piglet asked. "Are you having a lot of fun?"

"No," said Pooh thoughtfully, "doing nothing is not a LOT of fun."

"**I** was thinking," said Piglet, "maybe somebody needs us to help them with something."

"Something would be much better than nothing," agreed Pooh.

"Let's ask Owl," said Piglet. And with that, Pooh and Piglet set off for Owl's tree house.

"Owl!" called Pooh. "Do you need us to help you?"

"Most certainly!" declared Owl. "This dusting will get done more quickly with the help of two good friends."

Pooh and Piglet loved Owl's feather dusters –
they were great for tickling and cleaning.

"Thank you," said Owl, when his home was
shiny and clean. "Now I'm free to do nothing."

So Owl looked out of his window.

Pooh counted up his paws, but that didn't
take very long.

Piglet shifted in his seat. "Maybe Tigger
needs us to help
with something,"
he suggested.

"Tigger!" called Pooh. "Do you need us to help you?"

"Am I pleased to see you!" cried Tigger. "Picking up my toys would be much easier with three friends to help."

Piglet put away the toys on the lowest shelf. Pooh and Owl put away the toys on the middle shelves. Tigger bounced up high to put away the toys on the top shelf.

"We're a great team!" cried Tigger. "Let's go and see if Eeyore needs anything picked up."

"Eyore!" called Pooh.

"Oh!" everyone gasped. Eeyore's house had fallen down.

"It's much better as a house when it's upright," said Eeyore.

"What happened?" asked Pooh.

"Just what usually happens," said Eeyore. "The wind blew it down."

"Well," said Pooh, "it looks as if you need some help."

So Pooh, Piglet, Owl and Tigger helped Eeyore put his house together again. Then Owl showed the others how to tie it up with string – to make it stronger against the wind.

"The best way to build a house is with friends who help," said Eeyore. "Thank you!"

"You're welcome," said Pooh. "And now I think it's time for a little something, don't you?"

Pooh patted his tummy.
"A little something to eat,
I mean."

Tigger laughed. "Let's bounce
over and see what Rabbit's got cooking!"

"Do you have anything nice to eat?"
Pooh asked Rabbit.

"I've got a garden full of vegetables,"
sighed Rabbit. "But I've been pulling out
weeds all day, and I'm too tired to pick them."

"Do you need some help?" asked Pooh.

"Why, yes, that's exactly what I need!"
said a happy Rabbit.

"Just let me get everything organised," said Rabbit, who suddenly felt quite important and hardly tired at all.

"Pooh, you can pick potatoes, and Piglet, tomatoes. Tigger, you can pick the carrots, if Eeyore will pick the beans. And, Owl, if you would put all the vegetables in the wheelbarrow and bring them to me, I will wash them."

Soon big, juicy tomatoes, crunchy carrots, and snappy beans covered Rabbit's kitchen counter. Warm, steamy potatoes were cooking in a big pot.

"You have all been so helpful!" cried Rabbit. "To thank you, I want everyone to stay for supper!"

"Mmmmm, yummy," said Pooh.

After the meal was over, Pooh and Piglet sat in their Thoughtful Spot for a while and did . . . well . . . they did nothing at all!

"Whew! It feels good to rest," said Pooh.

"Yes," agreed Piglet. "Doing nothing is much more fun after a busy day of helping."

Pooh's Scrapbook

"Blah," said Tigger, "I hate rainy days. There's never anything to do."

"Blah," agreed Piglet.

"Well," said Pooh, "we could try to remember sunny days. That ought to make us feel more cheerful."

"I remember . . . making castles in the sand pit," tried Tigger.

" . . . gathering haycorns in a basket," said Piglet.

" . . . climbing the bee tree for honey," said Pooh.

"Ahhhhhhh," they all sighed. Now they were feeling worse!

"Oh, bother," said Pooh. "There must be something we can do. Think-think-think."

"Why don't we make a Sunny Day Scrapbook?" said Piglet.

"A book of scraps?" asked Pooh, who was thinking it sounded a little silly, though he didn't want to say so.

"No," said Piglet, "a colourful book, filled with special pictures and words – you know, scraps of memories."

"A memory book! What a clever idea," said Pooh.

They opened Pooh's cupboard and took out a stack of paper – all different colours.

They brought out paints and crayons for making pictures, and pencils for writing.

They brought out scissors and glue and ribbon for putting it all together.

"How do we start?" asked Tigger.

"I think we should tie the pages together first," said Piglet.

"Yes," agreed Pooh. "Then we can draw our memories and cut them out and glue them down on the pages."

Tigger counted out sheets of paper and then stacked them together neatly.

Pooh punched holes in the side of each sheet.

Piglet threaded the ribbon through the holes and tied it in a bow. Then they all sat down around Pooh's table and started making pictures of their favourite sunny-day things.

P iglet drew a picture of the time he and
Pooh went to Owl's house for tea. Pooh added
a paper teacup to the page.

Tigger drew Roo's jumping contest.
Then he cut out a "Best Bouncing" prize.

Pooh drew Rabbit's garden. He found some old seed packets to add to the page.

"Let's do more!" cried Piglet.

He drew a picture of everyone building Eeyore's new house.

Tigger added some cutout tools and a helpful drawing about how to build a house.

Tigger had fun painting.

Piglet drew a picture of his favourite game, Pooh Sticks. He added some leaves he'd saved from the day he won.

And Pooh drew a yummy picnic with friends!
He added lots of cutout honeypots.

Soon, their scrapbook was ready.

"This is SO nice, we should make a pretty cover for it," said Piglet. "Then it will be like a real book."

"Will these do?" asked Pooh, holding up two sheets of heavy paper.

"Yes," said Piglet. "But they're too big. I'll trim them so they're just a little bigger than our scrapbook paper."

When they were just right, Pooh punched three holes in each heavy sheet, to line up with the holes in the paper.

Tigger rethreaded the ribbon through all the holes and tied the bow again.

"Our Sunny Day Scrapbook!" read Piglet proudly, as he printed the title on the cover.

"Tiggers love rainy days," sighed Tigger, admiring their work.

"They're the best," agreed Piglet.

"Next time it's sunny," said Pooh, "let's make a Rainy Day Scrapbook."

"That's a great idea!" cried Tigger and Piglet together.

You Can Make a Scrapbook, Too!

A scrapbook can be about anything you like: a birthday party, a holiday, your family, pets, or something you dream about!

You could fill your scrapbook with anything you feel like! Here are some ideas.

Photographs, postcards or stamps.

Cinema or theatre tickets.

Pictures from magazines.

To decorate the cover, you could paint pictures, glue fabric down, or create a collage with cutout pictures and coloured paper.

Remember that you can put anything you want in your scrapbook, and decorate it exactly as you like! It's your special book to keep forever!

Pooh
Welcomes Winter

"Winter will be here soon," said Winnie the Pooh. "That's what Christopher Robin says."

"Who's Winter?" asked Piglet.

"The someone who is coming soon," said Pooh.

"Oh, a visitor!" said Piglet. "We should do something nice for him."

"We could give a party," said Pooh.

"What a grand idea," said Piglet.

"Come on," said Pooh. "Let's go and tell the others."

Outside, the cold wind was busy blowing the last leaf off the old oak tree. A few fluffy snowflakes rushed down Pooh's collar and settled behind Piglet's ears.

"It's hat and scarf weather," said Pooh.

"P-P-Pooh," shivered Piglet, "p-p-perhaps we should stay at home today and tell everyone about the p-p-party tomorrow."

"But the party will be over by then," said Pooh.

Pooh put on a hat and scarf. He wrapped a Pooh-sized scarf around little Piglet twice.

By the time the friends got to Kanga's house, they were so cold they had to stay for tea.

When they were finally warm enough to remember why they were there, Pooh said, "Winter is coming soon, and we're giving him a party."

"Hooray! A party!" cried Tigger.

"Let's go!" said Roo.

They opened the door. A pile of snow swooshed in and buried them. The wind was quiet. The Hundred-Acre Wood seemed to be snoozing under a blanket of white. Kanga, Piglet and Pooh, Tigger and Roo were under a white blanket, too.

They blinked.

"How will we get to the party?" asked Piglet. "The snow's so deep!"

"Don't worry," said Tigger, "we'll go by sledge!" They said goodbye to Kanga and off they swished.

Tigger and Pooh pulled. Piglet and Roo rode. Roo reached over the side and grabbed some snow to make snowballs. He piled them onto the sledge.

"These will make great presents for Winter," Roo said.

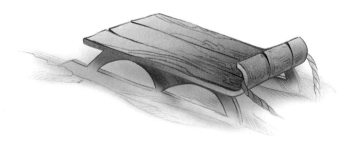

"Winter has arrived!" declared Owl, who had landed on a branch overhead. "I heard Christopher Robin say so."

"Oh!" cried Pooh. "Do you know where Winter is?"

"I haven't seen him myself," said Owl.

"We'll have to hurry and find him," said Pooh. He told Owl about the party. "Would you fly over and tell Rabbit and Gopher?"

"Don't forget Eeyore," whispered Piglet.

"And Eeyore," said Pooh.

"I'd be happy to oblige," said Owl.

As Owl flew off, Tigger and Pooh climbed onto the sledge with Piglet and Roo.

"Whooa!" they all shouted as they slid down the hill towards Christopher Robin's house to ask him where they could find Winter.

"There's Christopher Robin!" cried Roo.

Pooh called out, "Hellooo!"

Christopher Robin didn't answer.

"Oh, no!" cried Piglet. "Maybe he's frozen in the cold!"

"That's not Christopher Robin," said Tigger. "That's Winter!"

"Winter?" whispered Pooh. "But how do you know?"

"Tiggers always know Winter when they see him. That big white face – that carroty nose. Who else could he be?"

"Well," said Pooh, "he looks shy." He stumbled up to Winter. "How do you do?" he said. He shook Winter's stick hand. "I'm Pooh, and this is Tigger and Piglet and Roo."

Winter was very quiet.

Piglet nudged Pooh. "Tell him about the party."

"What party?" asked Pooh.

"You know," whispered Piglet, "HIS party."

"Oh, yes," said Pooh. "We are so happy to have you here, we are giving a party in your honour."

Winter didn't say anything.

"Oh d-dear," said Piglet. "He's frozen!"

"Quick!" said Tigger. "We'd better get him to the party."

Together they hoisted Winter onto the sledge.

Roo showed him the snowballs. "I made these just for you," he said.

Winter did not even look.

"He's in a bad way," said Tigger.

Tigger and Pooh pulled while Roo and Piglet pushed.

When they slid up to Pooh's house, the others were already there. Owl had hung a big sign over Pooh's door – WELCOME WINTUR.

Rabbit and Gopher were inside making steamy hot cocoa and honey carrot cake.

Pooh and Tigger wrestled Winter off the sledge.

"Give him the comfy chair by the fire!" ordered Rabbit. "Gopher, get him some cocoa!"

But still Winter didn't say a word. His carrot nose drooped. His stick hands fell.

"Oh, no!" cried Piglet.

"Maybe he's not the party type," said Eeyore.

"Our cocoa'sss making him sssick," whistled Gopher.

"What are we going to do?"cried Rabbit.

Just then Christopher Robin appeared.

"Has anyone seen my snowman?" he asked.

"No," said Pooh glumly, "but Winter is here. We brought him here for a special party."

"Winter's not a who, it's a what!" Christopher Robin laughed.

"What?" asked Pooh.

"My snowman!" said Christopher Robin.

"He's not Winter?" asked Pooh.

"No," said Christopher Robin. "Winter is the season – you know, cold snow and mistletoe. Warm fires and good friends."

Pooh scratched his nose thoughtfully. "Oh, I see," he said. "I am a bear of no brain at all."

"You're the best bear in all the world," said Christopher Robin. "Come on, we'd better get the snowman back outside before he melts."

"Oh d-dear," said Piglet. "I hope we haven't ruined him."

"Snowmen are easy to mend," said Christopher Robin.

They undrooped his nose and stuck his stick hands back in.

"Pooh," said Christopher Robin, "we can still have a party to celebrate winter. I think it's a wonderful idea!"

"Is it?" asked Pooh.

"Oh yes," said Christopher Robin. "Come on, let's have some fun!"

They threw Roo's snowballs. They took turns riding on Tigger's sledge. They made snow angels. They caught snowflakes on their tongues. They sang songs and danced around the snowman until they couldn't dance anymore.

"Everyone in for honey carrot cake and hot cocoa!" called Rabbit. They all gathered around the fire.

Christopher Robin gave Pooh a little hug. "Happy winter, Pooh," he said.

"Happy winter!" cried Pooh.

Be Patient, Pooh

COME TO POOH'S BIRTHDAY PARTY!

One morning Winnie the Pooh woke up thinking about cake and presents and balloons. It's not every day that a bear wakes up thinking of cake and presents and balloons. But today was Pooh's birthday, and his friends were giving him a party.

A birthday party for me, thought Pooh excitedly. I can't wait!

He shuffled over to his clock. "Is it time for my birthday party yet?" he asked.

Pooh's clock didn't say anything. The little hand pointed quietly at the eight and the big hand pointed at the twelve. Breakfast time, thought Pooh. That's always a good time.

He set out three pots of honey. "By the time I've finished these, it'll be almost time for my party," he said hopefully.

But when he'd licked the last drop of honey from the bottom of the last pot, it was still not time for his party.

Pooh did his stoutness exercises, twice.
But it was still not time for his party.

"I'd better go to Rabbit's house to see how the party is coming along," decided Pooh.
He hurried up the path.

"Everything's fine," said Rabbit, standing at his door and blocking Pooh's view. "The party will be ready at suppertime."

"Can I see my cake?" asked Pooh. He tried to look round Rabbit to find it.

"Not yet," said Rabbit. "Suppertime!"

Pooh sighed. It was not anywhere near suppertime yet. Maybe having a little company will help pass the time, thought Pooh.

He knocked at Piglet's door, and heard the sound of paper rustling inside.

"Don't come in yet!" cried Piglet. He finished tying a pink ribbon round Pooh's present and quickly hid it in the cupboard.

Then he called out, "You can come in now!"

"Can I see my present, Piglet? What do you think we'll do at the party, Piglet? Do you think Rabbit will put colourful roses on my cake? How much longer do you think it'll be, Piglet?" asked Pooh all in a big jumble.

He settled in Piglet's comfy chair. "It is nice to have company to talk to about all these things," said Pooh. "It helps pass the time in a friendly way, doesn't it?"

Piglet had opened his mouth and was trying to decide which question to answer first, when Tigger and Roo knocked at the door.

"Lunchtime!" cried Tigger as he and Roo bounced in.

Piglet looked at his clock. The big hand and the little hand were both pointing at the twelve.

"Lunchtime," said Pooh thoughtfully. "That's a lot closer to suppertime than breakfast time is, isn't it?"

"It's right NOW," said Tigger, who was quite hungry and had no idea which things were closer to what other things.

"Lunchtime is one of my favourite times of day," said Pooh. He helped Piglet and Tigger and Roo set the table.

As he was licking his last pot of honey clean, he sighed happily. "This is almost like a party right now."

"Oh, no," said Tigger, "a party has streamers and balloons and hats and ice cream and . . . "

Pooh thought about streamers and balloons and hats and ice cream (mmm, with plenty of honey) and cake and presents and . . . "Is it almost time for the party?" he asked.

"Oh, I hope not," said Piglet. "I promised to help Rabbit decorate."

"Me, too," said Tigger.

"And me, too, too," said Roo. Off they rushed.

P ooh went to see Christopher Robin.

"Why does it take SO long for a party to come?" he asked.

"It just SEEMS long, Pooh," said Christopher Robin. "When you have to wait, the best thing is to do something you really like because it makes the time go more quickly."

"What do bears like to do?" asked Pooh, hoping Christopher Robin could remind him.

"Well, I'm reading this great story about a pirate bear who's looking for buried treasure," said Christopher Robin. "Would you like me to read it to you?"

"Oh, would you?" said Pooh happily.

They snuggled together under a shady tree, and Christopher Robin read and read. Pooh forgot all about cake and presents and balloons. He closed his eyes and saw tall ships, rolling waves and buried treasure. They were just getting to "X marks the spot" when Christopher Robin thought he'd better check his watch.

The little hand pointed at the five, and the big hand pointed at the twelve. "Suppertime!" said Christopher Robin.

"You mean it's time for my party ALREADY?" cried Pooh.

Christopher Robin took Pooh's present from its hiding place and started off for Rabbit's house. "Come on, Pooh!" he called.

"Cake and presents and balloons! It's time, it's time, it's time!" sang Pooh as they walked along together.

Pooh was the first one to reach the door. Rabbit swung it open and shouted, "Happy birthday!"

Inside, Pooh saw his beautiful birthday cake with pink roses, and honeypots all wrapped in crinkly paper, and lots of colourful balloons, and streamers, and all his friends in party hats shouting, "Happy birthday, Pooh!"

"Oh!" cried Pooh. "Party time is my favourite time ever!"

Then Pooh hugged his good friends Piglet and Christopher Robin.

"And thanks to you," he whispered, "waiting was a great time, too."